The Mighty King
and the Small Creature

Norma J. McKayhan

Illustrations by
Marvin Alonso

Order this book online at www.trafford.com
or email orders@trafford.com

Most Trafford titles are also available at major online book retailers.

Illustrations by Marvin Alonso

Printed in the United States of America.

ISBN: 978-1-4669-1463-6 (sc)

978-1-4669-1462-9 (e)

Library of Congress Control Number: 2012907039

Trafford rev. 05/24/2012

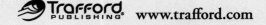 www.trafford.com

North America & international
toll-free: 1 888 232 4444 (USA & Canada)
phone: 250 383 6864 • fax: 812 355 4082

The Mighty King
and the Small Creature

Written by **Norma J. McKayhan**

DEDICATION

To my daughter who is the love of my life and to my Mother who loves me beyond measure

Stand up to your fears;
they are much smaller than you think!

The mighty King Levi rules his territory with a firm hand. He takes great effort in protecting his prides enormous region. All the other animals obey and respect him. So when he heard that there was unrest stirring in his domain, he wanted to see first hand what was going on.

Although he seldom leaves his chamber un-accompanied, the king went out to inspect his territory. He left his pride behind to venture on his own.

The mighty king was not afraid to roam alone because he knew his strength and power. He knew none of the other animals would dare challenge him. With his razor sharp claws and powerful jaw, he could destroy any creature with little effort.

As King Levi was roaming through his domain, he crossed paths with a small animal name Buckie. The king did not like small creatures like Buckie and roared to show his disapproval. He believed small creatures caused big problems in the jungle.

Buckie was afraid to be in the presence of the terrifying king. He knew the king ruled with a firm hand and did not like small animals like him. He trembled and feared he would be destroyed by this mighty beast.

After some time had passed, the mighty lion grew tired of taunting the small frightened creature, and asked "Why don't you stand up and fight? Stop whimpering about how afraid and helpless you are."

The poor, very frightened animal replied, "Mighty King Levi, if I had your strength, your size, and of course had your powers, I would not be so afraid. But until that day, I have to take what comes my way."

But a short time later, the small animal grew weary of being picked on. He gathered up enough courage to ask the mighty lion, "Sir, why do you hold me prisoner; why do you like taunting me? Is it because you can destroy me with a single slap of your paw?"

The mighty King Levi replied angrily, "If it were not for small, pesky creatures like you, who would I blame for the holes in the ground? Is it not your kind that destroys the plants and trees for food and shelter?"

The mighty king continued, "The jungle would be a safe place where I could roam and not step into holes made by creatures like you. Trees could grow tall and provide shade on a sunny day. Plants could give off a scent of sweetness in the air. The jungle would be just a better place to explore, if it was not for those like you."

Suddenly, the meek little animal realized, although the mighty king was of great strength and power, he could also be afraid of being destroyed by small creatures.

Then Buckie became very angry with King Levi because he blamed all the problems of the jungle on small animals instead of looking at other possibilities.

With a very bold voice, Buckie stood up and replied to the mighty king, "Sir, most of the holes in the jungle are uprooted trees caused by animals much larger than animals like me; most of the plants are eaten by animals much bigger than me. Also, most of the problems we have in the jungle are caused by animals like you!"

Thinking on what was said by the small creature, the mighty lion responded with a great roar and replied, "What you just said took courage."

He continued to say, "Although your words may be true, it's going to take time to get used to this way of thinking. But, I will admit that large and powerful creatures of the jungle are just as much at fault."

Buckie knew that his words made an impact on King Levi. It made the king think differently for the first time about the situations of the jungle.

Most importantly, Buckie realized that speaking up to the mighty king gave him confidence and a feeling of empowerment. He was not afraid to confront the mighty lion anymore, although he knew the king had the power to do away with him at any time.

But to Buckie's surprise, King Levi asked Buckie to join him as he seeks to find out why unrest was stirring in the region.

So it was that both mighty King Levi and the not so frightened Buckie found a new respect and understanding for the big and small creatures of the jungle.

A lesson to be learned from this story: Courage comes from within, so stand up to your fears; they are much smaller than you think!